RUFUS
and the
SCARY STORM
A BOOK ABOUT BEING BRAVE

By Lucy Bell
Illustrated by Michael Garton

First edition published 2018
Printed in the United States
23 22 21 20 19 18   1 2 3 4 5 6 7 8

Hardcover ISBN: 978-1-5064-3971-6

Illustrated by Michael Garton
Designed by Tim Palin Creative

Library of Congress Control Number: 2017960246

Sparkhouse Family
510 Marquette Avenue
Minneapolis, MN 55402
sparkhouse.org

SPARK
HOUSE
FAMILY
sparkhousefamily.org

Rufus always tried hard to be brave. He liked to think he was the strongest, bravest puppy in the world.

One day, Rufus was feeling especially strong.
He lifted a giant branch above his head.
His friends were impressed!

"Hey guys, watch this!" Rufus shouted as he held up two big rocks.

But his friends weren't paying any attention! Jo and Ava were staring up at the sky.

"Look, Rufus!" Ava called out.
"The sky is getting dark."

Jo pointed. "Clouds are moving in.
I think it's going to rain."

Rufus looked at the sky.

It *was* getting dark.

The clouds *were* moving in.

And now, the wind was howling too!

Just then, it thundered.

Rufus covered his ears.

Lightning flashed across the sky.

Rufus closed his eyes tight.

Rain started to fall.

One drop landed right on Rufus' nose.

More drops landed on his ears.

"Come on, Rufus!" Ava yelled. "We'd better get inside until this storm passes."

Ava and Jo ran giggling toward a stable.

Rufus ran after his friends.

But he wasn't giggling. He was whimpering.

Rufus hated storms.

Ava and Jo settled down on the ground in the stable to wait for the storm to pass.

Jo started to juggle some pebbles. Ava grabbed a stick to draw in the dirt.

But Rufus couldn't play.
He cowered in the corner.

Outside, the rain kept falling, the lightning kept flashing, and the thunder kept crashing.

Every time the thunder crashed,
Rufus's whole body trembled.

He looked at his friends.

"How can you play right now?"
he asked. "Aren't you afraid of the storm?"

"I'm not afraid of storms," said Ava. "But I'm afraid of other things. Like crossing the stream. I don't want to fall in and get wet!"

"Me too," Jo said. "I don't like
climbing up high. I'm afraid to fall!"

"I'm afraid of noisy storms," Rufus admitted. He was so ashamed. He wanted his friends to think he was big and brave.

But Ava and Jo didn't make fun of him.

"It's okay to feel afraid, Rufus," Ava said.
"Eveyone gets scared sometimes.
But God watches over us when we're afraid.
We can trust God!"

Rufus inched to the edge
of the stable and looked outside.

Dear God,

Sometimes I get afraid. Please help me to trust you when I'm scared.

Amen.

Rufus opened his eyes and looked at his friends. He felt a little better. Then he saw something leaning in the corner of the stable, and he got an idea.

"Look what I can do!" he said.

"Wow!" said Ava and Jo.

Rufus felt like the bravest puppy
in the world again!

ABOUT THE STORY

Rufus likes to think he's a brave puppy, but a loud storm scares him. His friends and a prayer help him learn that it's okay to be afraid, and that God is with him when he's scared.

DELIGHT IN READING TOGETHER

As you read, use an expressive voice to convey Rufus's transition from bravery to fear, and back to bravery again! When Rufus's friends share their different fears, ask your child what they're afraid of. The answers may surprise you!

ABOUT YOUNG CHILDREN AND FEAR

Fear can be a surprising and unpredictable emotion. Children might be unfazed by something we expect to scare them, while something we think is no big deal sends them running. Whatever your child's unique fears, don't shame or push them. Let them know that it's okay to be afraid—and then gently assure them that they're safe.

A FAITH TOUCH

Fear is a normal part of life. But we have a God who is with us in our fear, and who wants to keep us safe!

When I am afraid
I will trust in you.
        Psalm 56:3

SAY A PRAYER

Say the prayer Rufus said when he was feeling afraid.

Dear God,

Sometimes I get afraid. Please help me to trust you when I'm scared.

Amen.

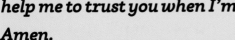